To Kim Faurot, friend and librarian extraordinaire.
From two of your biggest fans. —D. L. & M. W.

STERLING CHILDREN'S BOOKS
New York

An Imprint of Sterling Publishing
1166 Avenue of the Americas
New York, NY 10036

ISBN 978-1-4549-1574-4

Distributed in Canada by Sterling Publishing Co., Inc.
c/o Canadian Manda Group, 664 Annette Street
Toronto, Ontario, Canada M6S 2C8.
Distributed in the United Kingdom by GMC Distribution Services
Castle Place, 166 High Street, Lewes, East Sussex, England BN7 1XU
Distributed in Australia by Capricorn Link (Australia) Pty. Ltd.
P.O. Box 704, Windsor, NSW 2756, Australia

For information about custom editions, special sales, and premium and corporate purchases,
please contact Sterling Special Sales at 800-805-5489 or specialsales@sterlingpublishing.com.

Manufactured in China
Lot #:
2 4 6 8 10 9 7 5 3 1
05/16

www.sterlingpublishing.com

The artwork for this book was created using gouache.
Art direction and design by Merideth Harte.

by
DAVID LAROCHELLE

illustrated by
MIKE WOHNOUTKA

STERLING CHILDREN'S BOOKS
New York

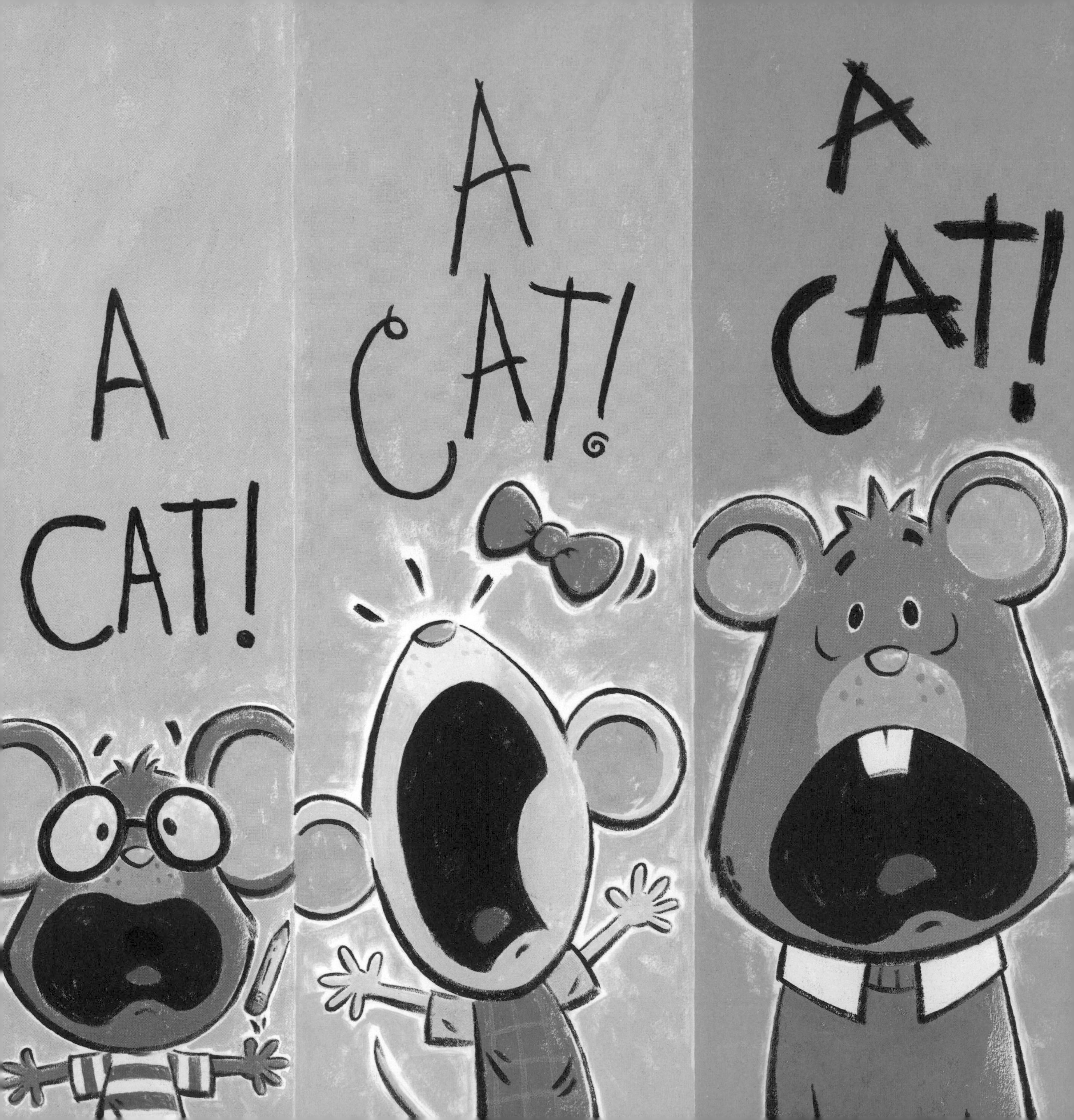
A CAT!
A CAT!
A CAT!

A cat?

IS this a cat?

This is NOT a cat!

THIS is a cat!

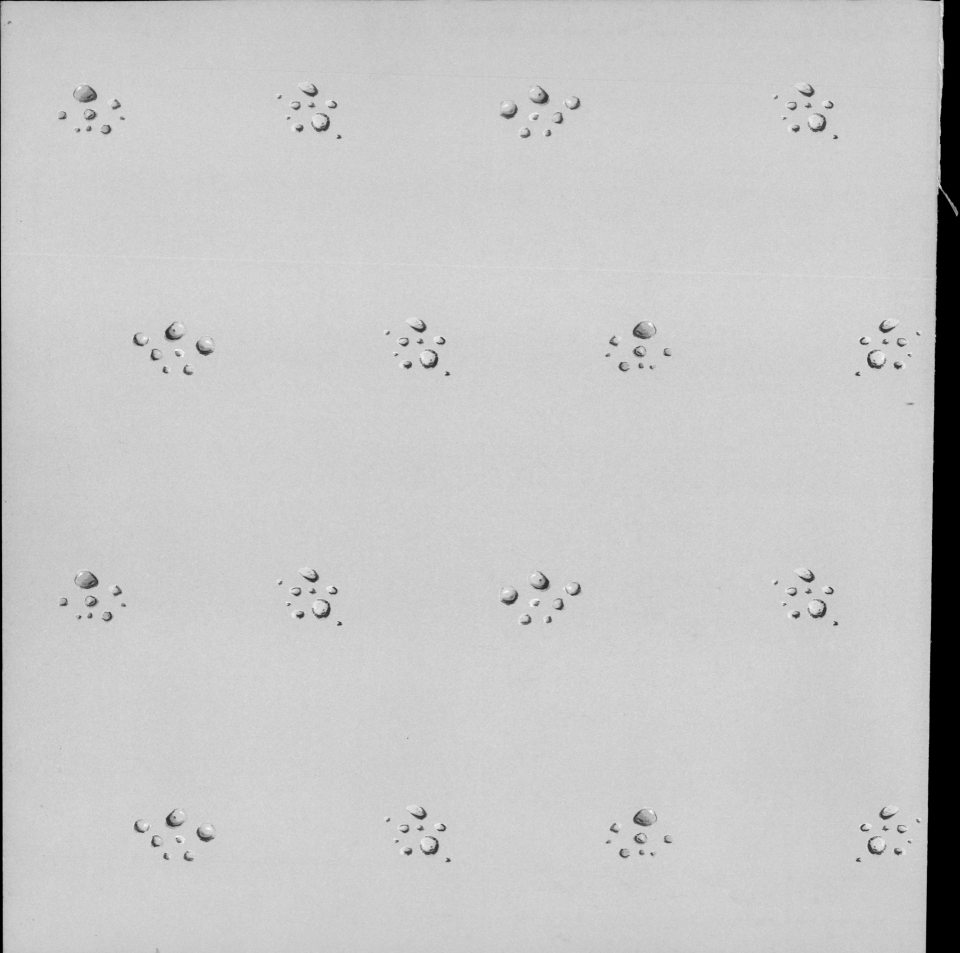